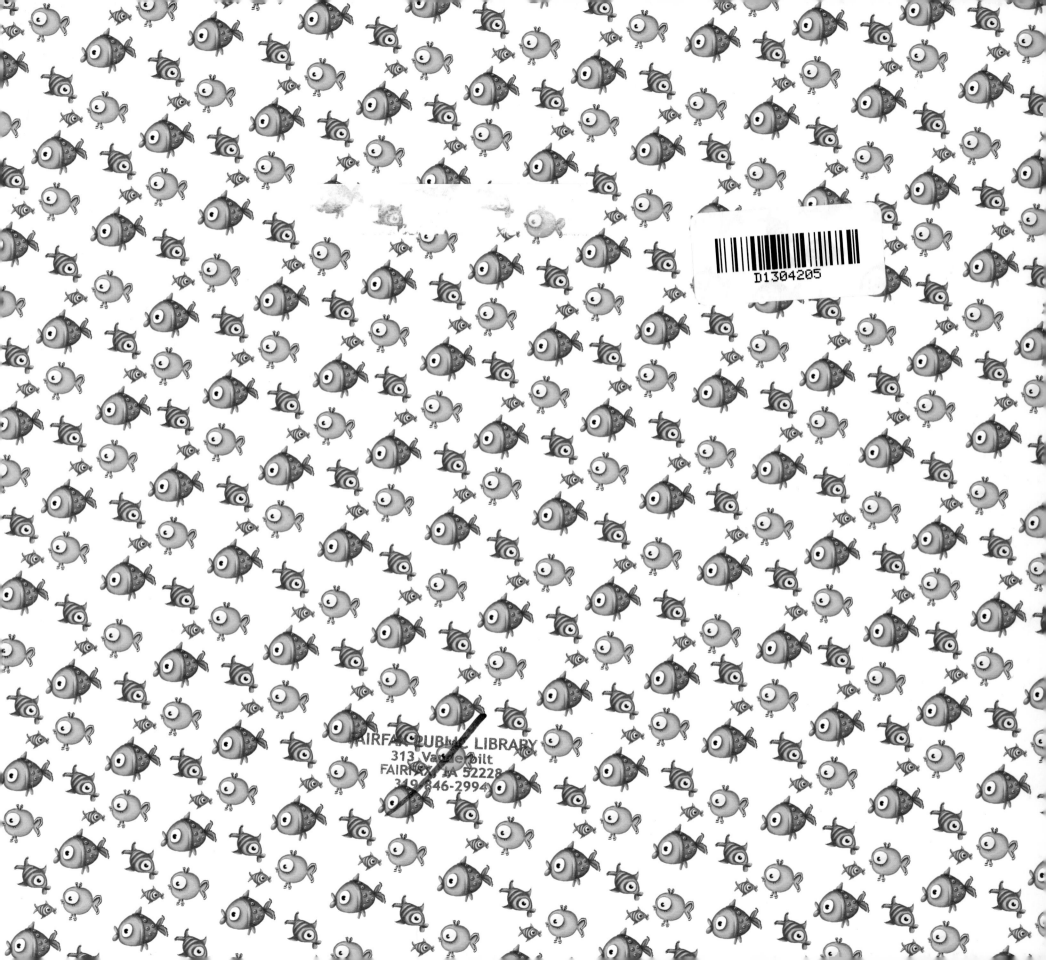

# Michael Recycle
## and
### Bootleg Peg

Written by Ellie Patterson

Illustrated by Alexandra Colombo

in support of the
Environmental Justice Foundation's (EJF)
Save the Sea campaign

When Michael went to visit,
one fateful Friday night,
the famous Neptune's Nibbles
for a tasty, fishy bite . . .

. . . he couldn't quite believe his eyes,
alas the ocean venue,
had tables bare with no one there . . .
and fish was off the menu!

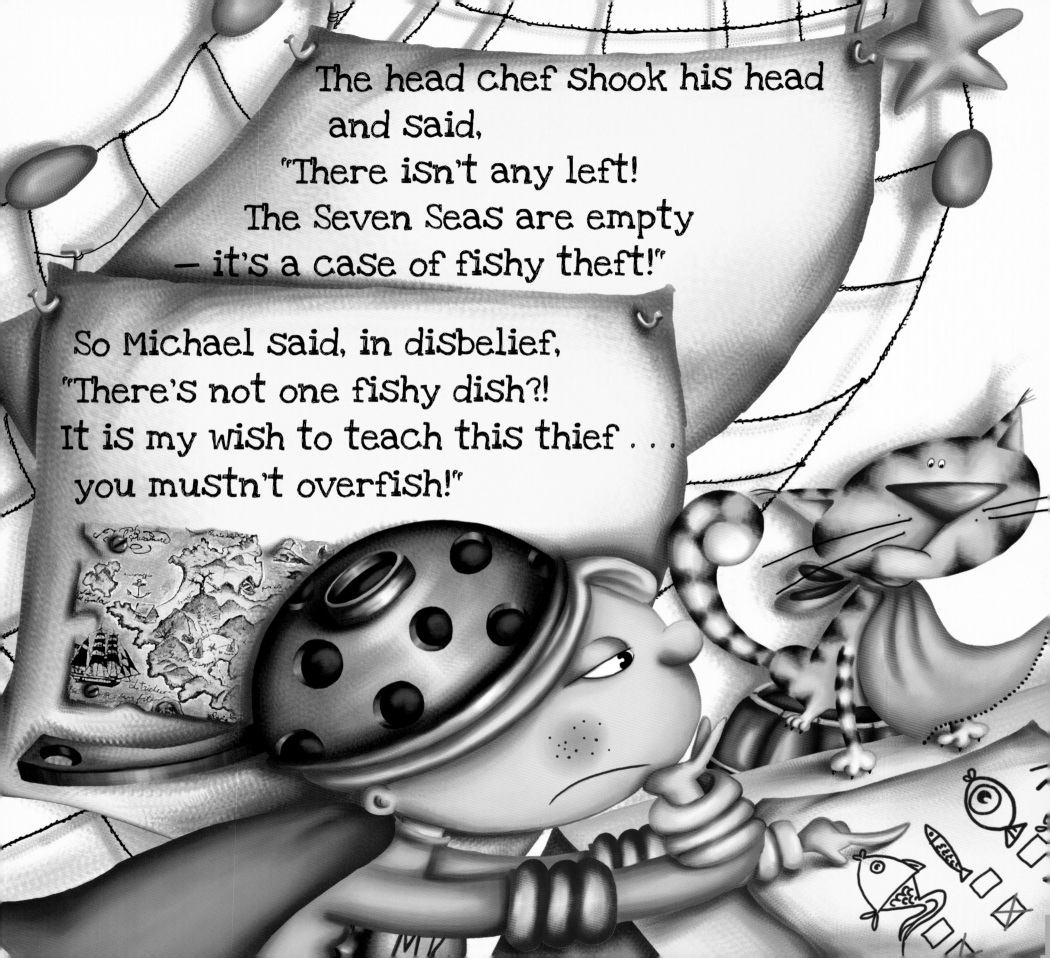

The head chef shook his head
and said,
"There isn't any left!
The Seven Seas are empty
— it's a case of fishy theft!"

So Michael said, in disbelief,
"There's not one fishy dish?!
It is my wish to teach this thief . . .
you mustn't overfish!"

Meanwhile, close to Africa,
the fearsome Bootleg Peg
gave orders to her gruesome crew
and Captain Toothless Greg.

A wicked witch upon the waves,
she was the ocean's curse.
For stealing fishes from the sea,
there was no pirate worse!

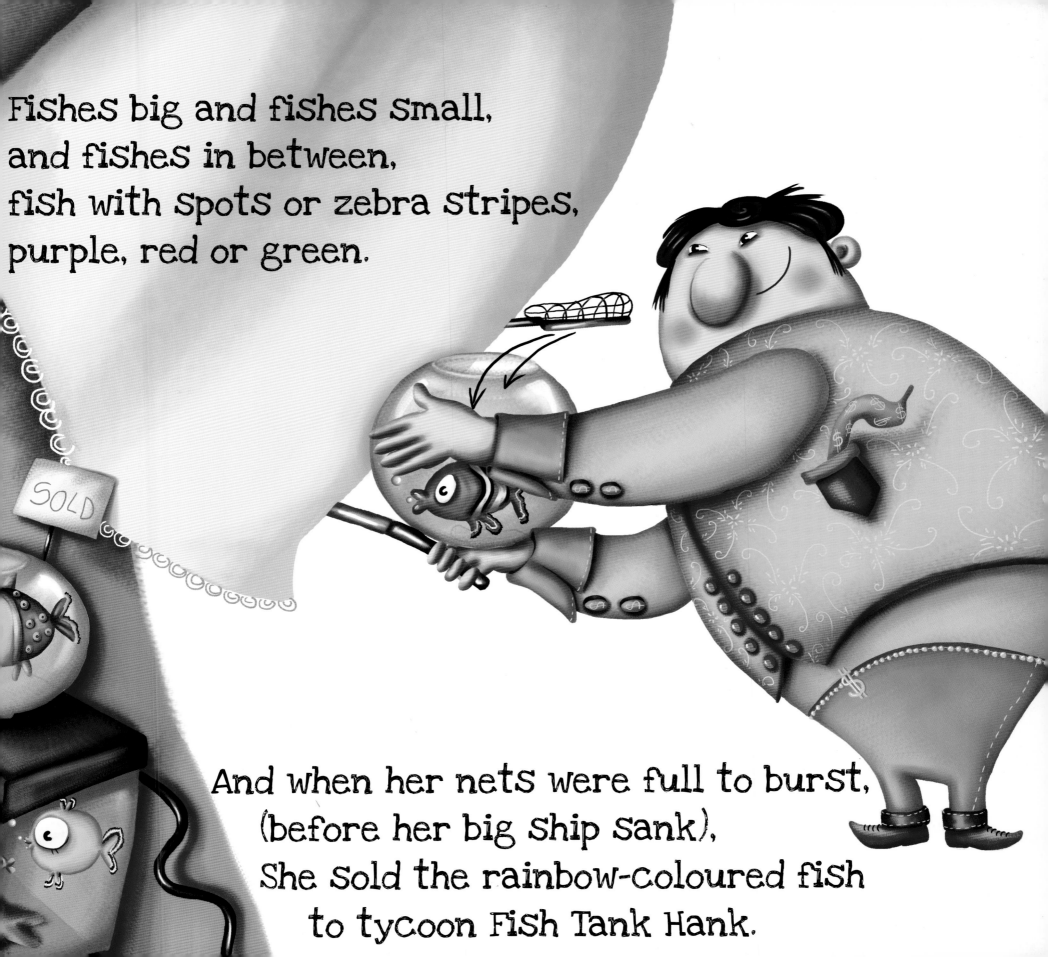

Fishes big and fishes small,
and fishes in between,
fish with spots or zebra stripes,
purple, red or green.

And when her nets were full to burst,
(before her big ship sank),
She sold the rainbow-coloured fish
to tycoon Fish Tank Hank.

But Peggy's nets not only caught
the rainbow-coloured fishes,
they also caught the types of fish
in Neptune's Nibbles dishes!

So Michael soared above the waves
to see who it could be,
when he spotted that the fish had left
a message in the sea!

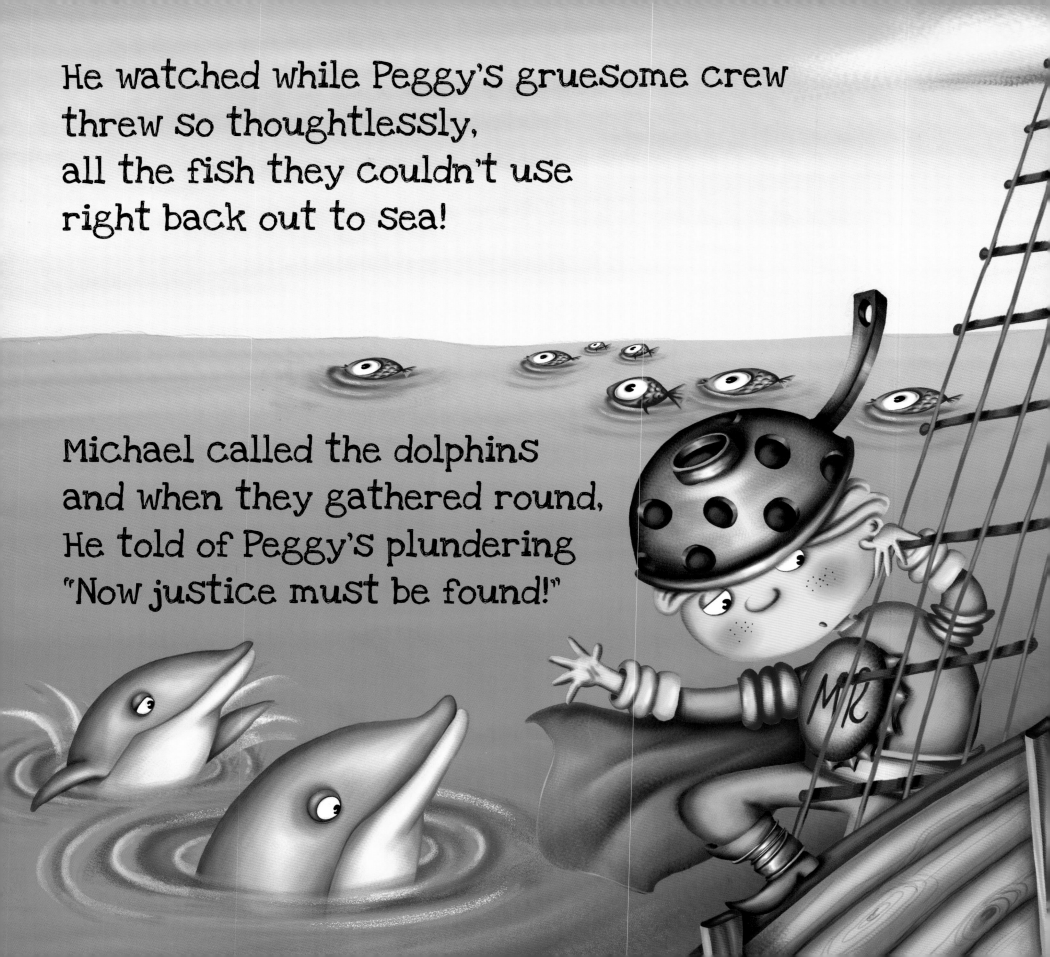

He watched while Peggy's gruesome crew
threw so thoughtlessly,
all the fish they couldn't use
right back out to sea!

Michael called the dolphins
and when they gathered round,
He told of Peggy's plundering
"Now justice must be found!"

"I need your help, my fine-finned friends,
in finding Ol' Big Blue.
The wisest whale in all the world . . .
he'll know just what to do!"

SAVE
OUR
SEAS!

Now Ol' Big Blue was peaceful
but when he heard the crime,
he flipped his tail and shouted,
"Let's go — there's not much time!"

That Bootleg Peg, she must be stopped!
It's time for us to act . . .
So dolphins, at the ready!
And Michael — on my back!"

So Michael rode the Seven Seas
atop of Ol' Big Blue,
and when he came to Peggy's ship,
Big Blue knew what to do.

He tossed and turned and twisted
and slapped his awesome tail,
to cause a mighty maelstrom
with waves quite off the scale.

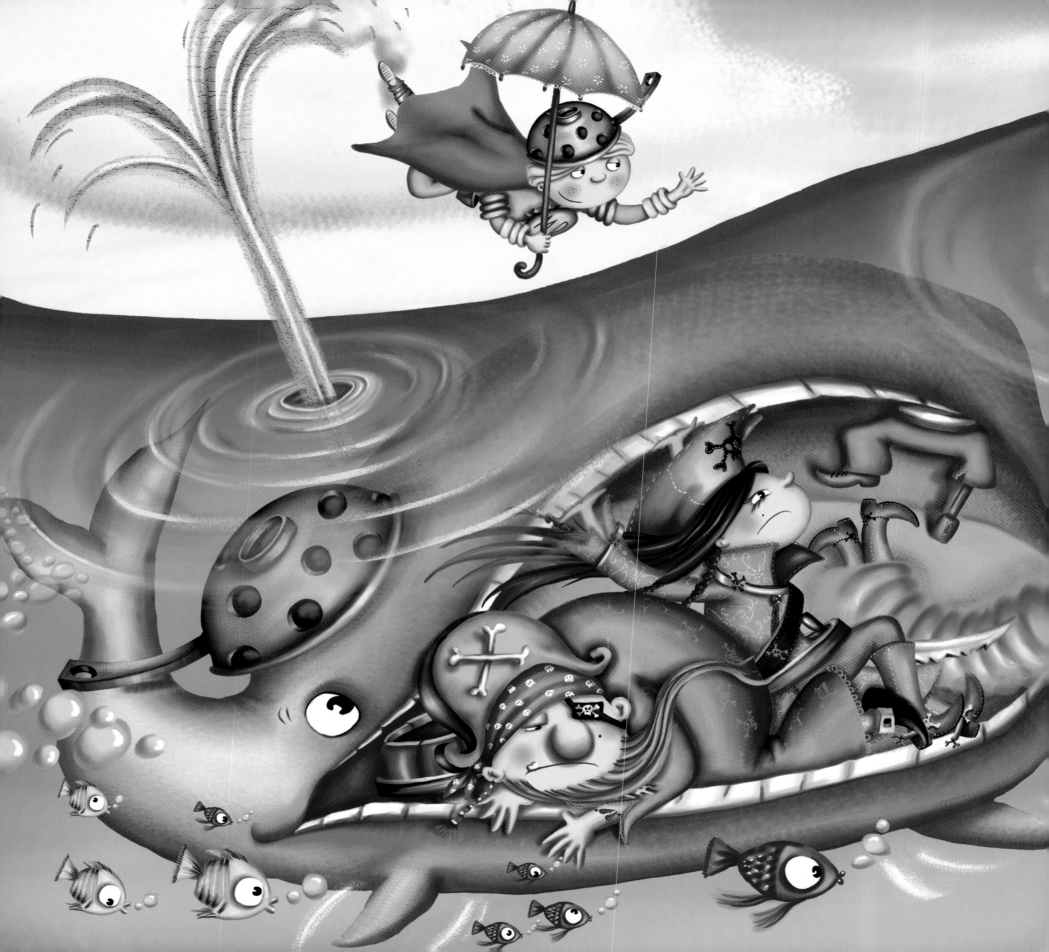

"Bootleg Peg!" cried Michael,
"This is your red alert!
Stop your overfishing . . .
or be a shark's dessert!"

But still the ship kept sailing
despite the frightened crew.
So in one go Blue swallowed it,
and Greg and Peggy too!

And then in one almighty breath
he spat the thieving pair
on to a desert island . . .
a thousand miles from there!

And since there wasn't much to eat —
it was as Michael wished —
Peggy learnt that to survive
she mustn't overfish!

Now back at Neptune's Nibbles
the menu's all brand new,
with fishy treats for Michael . . .
. . . and some for old friends too!

# ENVIRONMENTAL JUSTICE FOUNDATION

## Protecting People and Planet

**The Environmental Justice Foundation** (EJF) is a British charity working internationally to protect people and our shared planet.

EJF works to protect fish, endangered wildlife including sharks, turtles and dolphins, and to care for the people who most depend on our global seas and oceans for their food and incomes. EJF's priority is to end illegal fishing that is stealing fish from some of the world's poorest countries.

A donation from the sale of this book goes directly to support EJF's projects working with fishing communities and conservation groups in West Africa.

EJF, 1 Amwell Street, London, EC1R 1UL, UK.
info@ejfoundation.org • www.ejfoundation.org
EJF is a registered charity in the UK, number 1088128.

Find out more about EJF, and the Save the Sea campaign which this book supports, at
**www.ejfoundation.org/oceans/michaelrecycle**

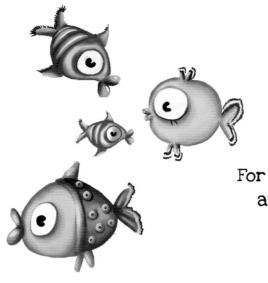

For Andy, everyone at EJF
and the fishermen of
Sierra Leone.
E.P.

To Roby & Bot who are
part of my family.
A.C.

www.idwpublishing.com
ISBN: 978-1-61377-708-4
16  15  14  13    1  2  3  4  5